Eddie Orlando was born and raised in Brooklyn ,New York . He started his career as a bricklayer and later worked in the airline cargo industry at Flying Tigers .Ed 's love for nature began when he would go hiking and fishing in the beautiful Adirondack Mountains. He enjoys spending time working on his garden and has won numerous awards in his community for his landscape designs. He currently lives in St James, NY with his dog Rocco and has two daughters and seven grandchildren. He enjoys cooking and embracing many Italian recipes he grew up with as a young boy.

Alysia Stern has been writing since the age of nine. She has taken her rhythmic gift and captured the hearts of children with her indie-published books "Don't Eat the Crayons" and "Good Friends Are Hard to Find". Alysia spends her free time rescuing and fostering dogs for a non-profit organization, feeding the homeless on Long Island and in New York City, and entertaining local senior citizens with her talents. She is the mother of twins and enjoys painting and finding hidden gems at thrift shops.

Emily Penna is a student at Smithtown High School East. Her love of drawing started at a very young age. She won the Smithtown Children's library card design when she was 10 years old. Emily enjoys skiing, biking and spending time with her family and friends. Next year she plans to go to college and pursue a career in computer graphic design. It was an honor for her to illustrate this book for her grandfather in memory of her grandmother.

Life is an adventure. What you think is the
end is only the beginning. Remember, wishes
do come true.

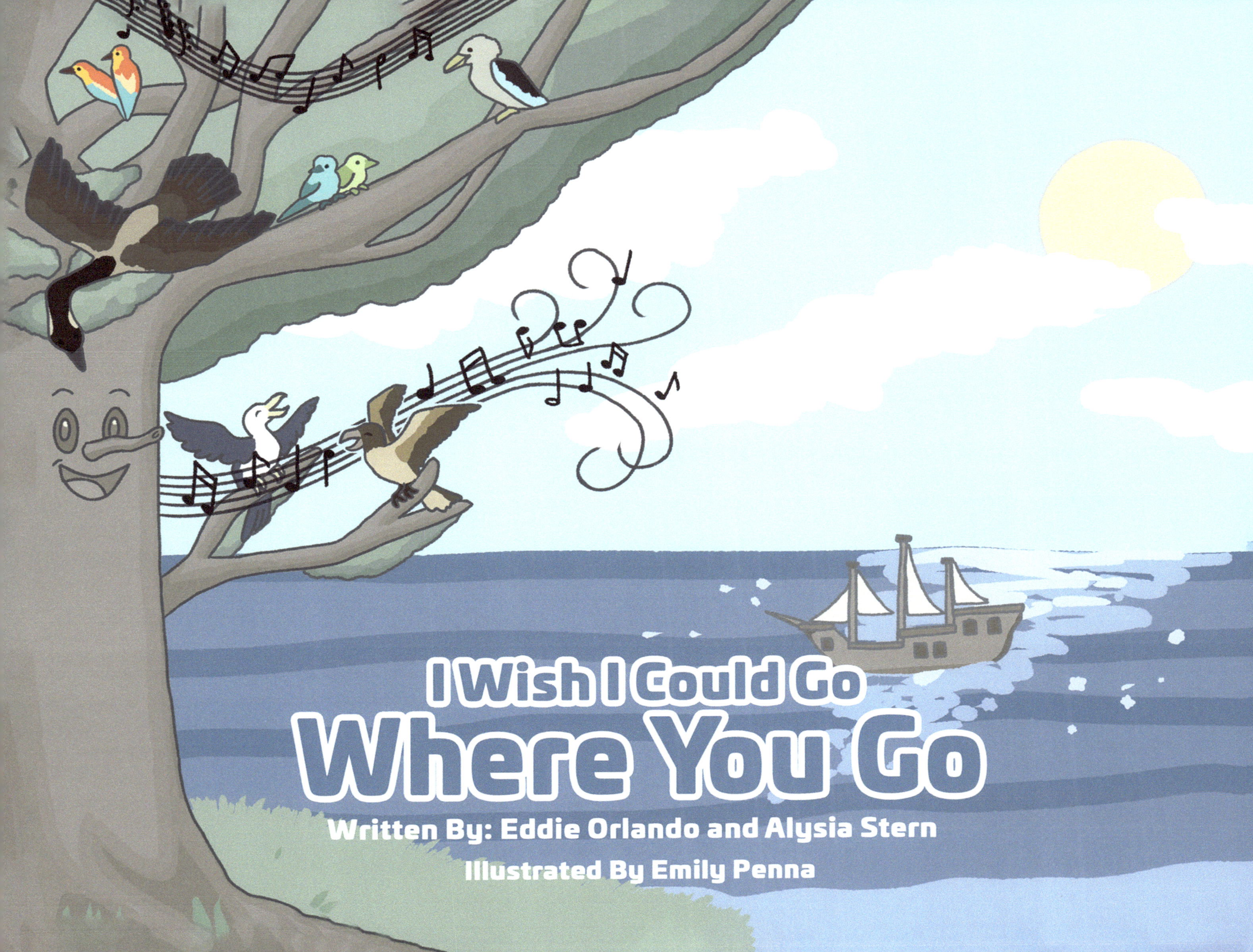

I Wish I Could Go
Where You Go
Written By: Eddie Orlando and Alysia Stern
Illustrated By Emily Penna

Copyright © Eddie Orlando and Alysia Stern (2020)
Illustrated by Emily Penna

Ordering Information
Quantity sales: Special discounts are available on quantity purchases by corporations, associations, and others. For details, contact the publisher at the address below.

Publisher's Cataloging-in-Publication data
Orlando, Eddie and Alysia Stern
I Wish I Could Go Where You Go

ISBN 978-1-80623-145-4 (Paperback)
ISBN 978-1-80623-146-1 (Hardback)
ISBN 978-1-80623-144-7 (ePub e-book)

www.audiobookpublishingservices.com

First Published (2020)
Audiobook Publishing Services
633 West Fifth Street, 26th and 28th Floors
Los Angeles, CA 90071
USA

info@audiobookpublishingservices.com

+1 213-871-1303
+1 210-888-0079

This is book is being dedicated to the memory of Eddie's wife, Joyce Orlando.
They were married for 55 years.

Eddie and Alysia would like to thank Eddie's daughters Debbie and Donna and Alysia's husband Cris
for helping us and supporting us through the journey.

For years and years
I stood so tall
With leaves and twigs
From spring through fall.
Planted firm
Through snow and drought
Never a chance
to Move about.

The one thing that stayed
were my friends with
their feathers
They sat on my branches,
And told tall tales of pleasure.
Day in and day out
They stopped by to chat
About the places they've flown
And the places they've sat.

And I whispered to myself, "I wish
I could go where they go."
A sadness I felt
For no stories I told

I just listened and cried
Over time I grew old.
"I'm stuck. I can't move
My roots keep me here
I'm just a large perch for
Birds, bugs, and deer."

Yet, day in and day out
They flew by to chat
and told me their adventures
and where they were at.
Then one bright sunrise
They all flew away
Not one feathered friend
Had wanted to stay.
The forest became quiet
Men with saws were all around
The next thing I knew
I was knocked to the ground.

Then placed on a truck
And driven in to town,
Sent to a saw mill
And painted dark brown.

"What is going on?"
I needed my friends
Their stories of adventures
I missed to no end.
I was brought to the water
And made into a mast
I stood firmly tall
Out to sea I was cast.

Across blue salty oceans,
Cold wind in my face
The sights that I saw
Brought me comfort and grace.
Like Magellan and Vespucci
I could sail and be free.
Like Drake and John Smith
I could navigate the sea.

From the Artic, to the Atlantic
To the Indian and Pacific
This new life abroad
Is just so terrific.
And Then,
One cold rainy day
While tied to a dock
I heard a commotion.
My mouth dropped in shock.
"Old friend, Is it you?
Have we found you by the sea?"
My friends had flown by, this time
To listen to me.

About Africa and Asia
Europe and Mexico
They listened to my adventures
about the places I now go.
They perched on my spar
Ate worms off the rudder
They sat by my bow
It was a day like no other.

The top sails were smiling
The port was laughing too
They loved my friend's tales
And this time, I DID TOO.
They whispered to me, "Now you
can go where we go."

Now day in and day out
They stop by to chat
About the places I have sailed
and the places they've sat.

And once in a blue moon
They sail along with me
And we pass the old stump
That was me, when I was a tree,
by the sea.

Always Believe!

www.ingramcontent.com/pod-product-compliance
Lightning Source LLC
Chambersburg PA
CBHW040130180726
48295CB00004B/95